Please return/renew this item by the last date shown.
Item may also be renewed by the internet*

https://library.eastriding.gov.uk

* Please note a PIN will be required to access this service
- this can be obtained from your library.

Winston Wallaby
Can't Stop Bouncing

by the same authors

Creating Autism Champions
Autism Awareness Training for Key Stage 1 and 2
Joy Beaney
Illustrated by Haitham Al-Ghani
ISBN 978 1 78592 169 8
eISBN 978 1 78450 441 0

From Home to School with Autism
How to Make Inclusion a Success
K.I. Al-Ghani and Lynda Kenward
Illustrated by Haitham Al-Ghani
ISBN 978 1 84905 169 9
eISBN 978 0 85700 408 6

Learning About Friendship
Stories to Support Social Skills Training in Children with
Asperger Syndrome and High Functioning Autism
K.I. Al-Ghani
Illustrated by Haitham Al-Ghani
ISBN 978 1 84905 145 3
eISBN 978 0 85700 348 5

also part of K.I. Al-Ghani's children's colour story books series

The Green-Eyed Goblin
What to do about jealousy − for all children
including those on the Autism Spectrum
K.I. Al-Ghani
Illustrated by Haitham Al-Ghani
ISBN 978 1 78592 091 2
eISBN 978 1 78450 352 9

The Disappointment Dragon
Learning to cope with disappointment (for all children and
dragon tamers, including those with Asperger syndrome)
K.I. Al-Ghani
Illustrated by Haitham Al-Ghani
ISBN 978 1 84905 432 4
eISBN 978 0 85700 780 3

The Panicosaurus
Managing Anxiety in Children Including
Those with Asperger Syndrome
K.I. Al-Ghani
Illustrated by Haitham Al-Ghani
ISBN 978 1 84905 356 3
eISBN 978 0 85700 706 3

The Red Beast
Controlling Anger in Children with Asperger's Syndrome
K.I. Al-Ghani
Illustrated by Haitham Al-Ghani
ISBN 978 1 84310 943 3
eISBN 978 1 84642 848 7

Winston Wallaby
Can't Stop Bouncing

*What to do about hyperactivity in children
including those with ADHD, SPD and ASD*

K.I. Al-Ghani and Joy Beaney

Illustrated by Haitham Al-Ghani

Jessica Kingsley Publishers
London and Philadelphia

First published in 2018
by Jessica Kingsley Publishers
73 Collier Street
London N1 9BE, UK
and
400 Market Street, Suite 400
Philadelphia, PA 19106, USA

www.jkp.com

Library of Congress Cataloging in Publication Data
A CIP catalog record for this book is available from the Library of Congress

British Library Cataloguing in Publication Data
A CIP catalogue record for this book is available from the British Library

ISBN 978 1 78592 403 3
eISBN 978 1 78450 761 9

Printed and bound in China

This book is dedicated to the memory of a dear husband and devoted father, Ahmed Mohammed I. Al-Ghani, and to our own little bouncer, Zeyad.

Kay

To my lovely daughters, Katharine and Joanne. Thank you for all your encouragement.

Joy

Introduction

Having a child with hyperactivity can be bewildering, frustrating and, of course, exhausting.

This is the child who is constantly fidgeting and unable to sit still.

The child who loves rough-and-tumble play, climbing, running, leaping and jumping, even in the most inappropriate places.

The child who constantly bumps and crashes into objects and people, seemingly unaware of personal space, at a time when other children of the same age understand it well.

The child who may have a high pain threshold and who enjoys the tightest of bear hugs.

The child who seems to crave the speedy, the spinning, the intensity of movement.

The child who likes nothing better than to fling off clothes and shoes.

The child of nature, at home with animals and the great outdoors.

The child who may need to touch people and things, often to the point of embarrassment.

The child who finds it hard to concentrate and thrive at school.

If this is your child and you were offered a magic potion that would dampen down this hyperactive system and restore peace and tranquillity, you may be tempted to take it, and no one would blame you. However, if you took a few minutes to understand how this may affect their perception of the world, you may be more reticent and exhaust other strategies first. Might it be better to train your child to recognise their sensory needs and give them tools and strategies to work with? Why not celebrate the positive aspects of hyperactivity? Nurture and train the speed and agility that may one day be honed into the next Olympian.

Winston Wallaby
Can't Stop Bouncing

Winston Wallaby, like most wallabies, was an excellent bouncer.

However, Winston just couldn't sit still.

Winston bounced when he was happy.

He bounced when he was sad.

He bounced when he was hungry.

He bounced when he was mad.

Winston bounced on the sofa,

He bounced on the chairs,

He bounced in the hallway,

He bounced up the stairs.

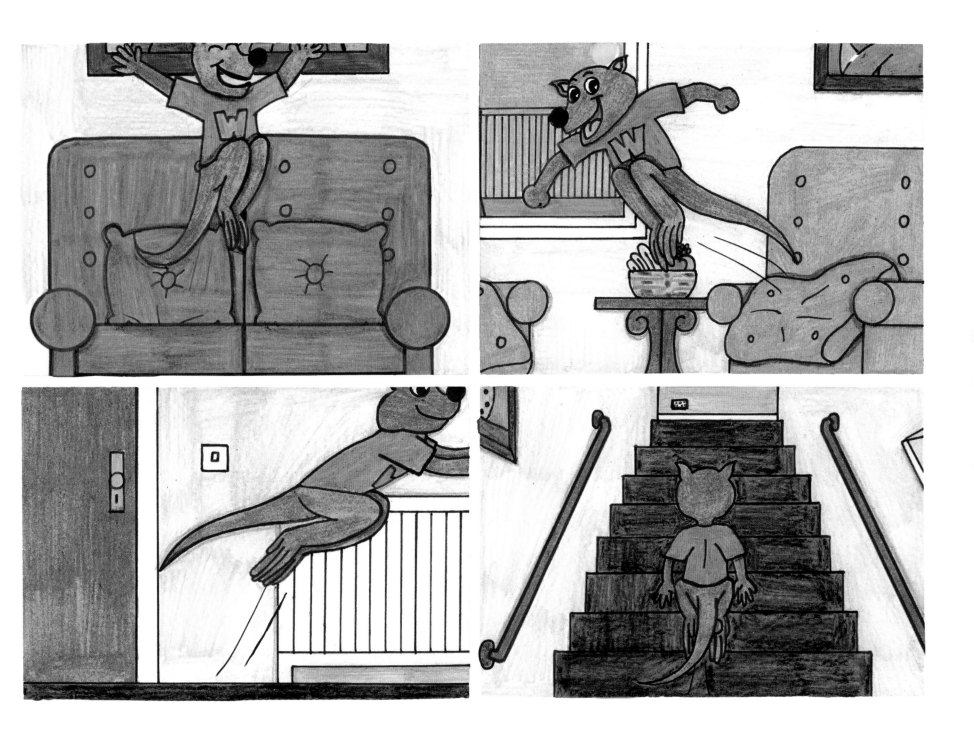

Winston bounced in the garden,

He bounced in the store,

He bounced on every windowsill,

He bounced through every door.

In fact, the only time Winston stopped bouncing was when he finally fell asleep!

At first light of dawn, Winston jumped out of bed for a whole new day of bouncing.

Winston's family had got used to his non-stop bounciness.

His mummy learned to put away breakables when Winston was around.

His daddy learned to put away his tools.

Granny and Grandpa learned to stay clear if Winston was in full bounce.

It was almost time for Winston Wallaby to be starting school.

Mummy Wallaby told him he would need to take care.

Daddy Wallaby told him he must learn to sit in a chair.

Granny Wallaby told him he must listen to his teacher.

Grandpa Wallaby told him, "Don't be such a bouncy creature!"

Winston started school one bright Monday morning.

He was very excited as Mrs Calm, his teacher, told the class to sit and listen for their names.

Winston tried very hard to remember what his family had told him. *"I won't bounce, I won't bounce, I won't bounce…"* Winston whispered to himself.

However, he forgot to listen for his name and a poke in the ribs by William Wallaby, sitting next to him, made him bounce right out of his seat, knocking over a pencil pot.

All the pupils laughed.

Mrs Calm frowned at the class and told Winston to sit down on his chair.

Winston tried to sit quietly and listen to his teacher.

"I won't bounce, I won't bounce, I won't bounce…" Winston whispered to himself.

Mrs Calm was telling the pupils about her classroom rules. They were all going to practise lining up and walking round the school sensibly.

"Winston! Winston!" called Mrs Calm sharply.

Winston looked up and was surprised to see everyone lined up by the door.

"Winston, what did I just tell everyone to do?" she asked him.

He had been concentrating so hard on not bouncing that he hadn't heard.

Winston's face went quite red and he felt everyone's eyes on him. He was so relieved when it was playtime and he could finally escape the classroom.

Winston raced out into the playground and bounced round and round joyfully. It felt good to be out in the fresh air.

He was so excited that he bumped into some of the pupils. He even knocked over a little wallaby called Wendy, causing her to cry out.

Winston was truly sorry but, although Wendy wasn't hurt, some of the other wallabies were angry with him. They gathered around Wendy and helped her up.

Winston felt so sad and sorry that it made him bounce even more.

After playtime and for the rest of the school day Winston had to sit by Mrs Calm's desk. He noticed some of the pupils whispering to each other and pointing at him.

He had tried so hard to be still and he really wanted Mrs Calm to be pleased with him, she smiled so kindly… But he just wished he didn't need to sit by her desk − it was so embarrassing.

That first day passed quickly enough, but Winston had broken his pencil twice, overturned his chair three times and spilled a whole pot of counting bricks all over the floor.

Mrs Calm smiled sweetly and told Winston not to worry − the first day of school was always hard and tomorrow was a new day.

The next morning was Tuesday.

Mrs Calm was waiting at the school gates to greet everyone.
She smiled at Winston.

"I won't bounce, I won't bounce, I won't bounce…" Winston whispered
to himself.

When he got inside, there was a round rubbery cushion and a little
waistcoat on his seat. Mrs Calm said these things would help him to
sit still and listen.

The waistcoat was very heavy and Winston felt a bit silly wearing it,
but he did like the feel of it. The little cushion was very comfy.

Mrs Calm told the class about Winston's cushion and waistcoat. She told
them he needed a bit of extra help to stop him being so bouncy.

"I won't bounce, I won't bounce, I won't bounce…" Winston whispered to himself.

For the next fifteen minutes Winston sat calmly and answered his name when the register was called. He was able to put up his hand and tell his teacher the names of the days of the week.

Mrs Calm smiled so sweetly at Winston that he felt as light as a feather and he bounced right out of his seat, almost landing on Mrs Calm's toes. Somehow, he could not feel the weight of the waistcoat anymore.

Mrs Calm removed the waistcoat and told Winston to bounce three times around the edges of the playground and then come back inside.

When Winston returned, all the pupils were in a circle on the floor ready for story time.

Mrs Calm told Winston to sit on his special cushion and then she draped a little blanket over his knees and put a heavy snake toy around his shoulders. All the children laughed and Mrs Calm told them that these things would help Winston to sit still so he could listen to the story properly.

Winston felt a bit silly, but he had to admit they did feel good.

"I won't bounce, I won't bounce, I won't bounce…" Winston whispered to himself.

Winston was able to sit calmly and listen to a story about a dingo called Racer, who loved to run.

After story time, Mrs Calm told the children they would be doing some painting. She had set out all the paint pots, brushes and water.

Winston felt so excited that he bounced right off his cushion. The snake and the lap blanket fell to the floor and, before Winston could stop himself, he bounced over to the table and upset one of the water pots. The water splashed over William, who was sitting nearby. William wasn't hurt, but he was very wet and not very happy.

The pupils started to laugh and Mrs Calm told everyone to be quiet. Then she told Winston to bounce five times around the playground before coming back into class.

When Winston returned, he saw that all the pupils had started their paintings, and Mrs Calm had prepared an easel for him to paint at so he didn't need to sit down.

Winston put on the heavy waistcoat again and Mrs Calm gave him an old jacket to wear and an especially heavy paintbrush. Winston liked the feel of it in his hand.

"I won't bounce, I won't bounce, I won't bounce…" whispered Winston to himself.

Winston painted a lovely picture of Racer, the dingo from the story.

Mrs Calm was very pleased with him. "What a lovely painting, Winston, well done! Is it easier for you to work standing up?" she asked him curiously.

"I think it is," said Winston.

"Then I think we will get a higher table, just for you," she said kindly.

When painting was over, it was time for P.E. and Mrs Calm set up a number of activities. There were skipping ropes, plastic hoops and carpet squares laid out around the playground.

The pupils had to count how many times they could skip or spin the hoops around their waists before stopping. Then they had to hop from square to square around the playground.

Winston wasn't very good at the hoops but he was the champion carpet hopper! If only school could be like this all day, he thought wistfully. He loved the great outdoors and all the wallabies laughed and bounced for joy in the summer sunshine.

The next day was Wednesday.

"I won't bounce, I won't bounce, I won't bounce…" Winston whispered to himself as he entered the classroom.

Winston saw that Mrs Calm had made him his own timetable with pictures showing what he would be doing throughout each day. After each activity there was an exercise picture. Winston learned that this meant after every bit of classwork he was to go for a bounce around the playground.

At playtime, Mrs Calm told Winston to stay close to the edges of the playground so he wouldn't bump into the other pupils. Wendy and William asked if they could join him and they bounced around together. Soon other wallabies joined them and Winston thought it such fun.

However, Winston had been so excited to be leading the little group of wallabies that he didn't hear the bell for end of playtime. When he looked round he saw he was all alone, everyone else had gone inside.

By the time Winston got back to class, he had missed Mrs Calm telling the children about the number work they had to do. He was worried she would be angry with him.

"I won't bounce, I won't bounce, I won't bounce…" Winston whispered to himself.

However, Winston knew that he would bounce. He simply could not stop himself.

As bounced from his chair, large, fat tears rolled down his cheeks. He could not understand why all the other wallabies could manage to sit and learn and he couldn't.

He bounced with a heart full of sadness.

Winston's classmates were very concerned and they looked to Mrs Calm.

Mrs Calm took Winston over to her rocking chair. She sat him on her knee and gently rocked him to and fro. She told Winston that his body was still trying to sort out where he was and that it would take time for him to learn how to be still and listen.

When Winston was calm again, she spoke to all the class and explained that Winston needed extra help so he could learn. Winston's tears had upset the pupils and they felt bad for having laughed at him so much.

When Mrs Calm asked the class if they would like to join Winston in doing some activities that would help, they all smiled and nodded their approval.

First, they had to sit with hands on heads and push down into their chair, counting backwards slowly from five to one.

Then they put their hands on either side of their chair and raised their bottoms in the air for as long as they could. The pupils thought this was great fun.

Every fifteen minutes, Mrs Calm shook a little shaker and all the class had to stand up, jump on the spot ten times and then sit down with hands on heads, pushing down into their chair to a count of 5, 4, 3, 2, 1.

Winston was so happy to see all the wallabies enjoying these little exercise breaks.

After school that day, Mrs Calm asked Winston's mummy if she could speak to her.

Mummy Wallaby felt very worried. She sat Winston on her knee and, holding him tightly, gently bounced him up and down.

Mrs Calm told Winston's mummy that Winston had been trying very hard not to bounce in class, but he needed some extra help. She gave her a list of activities that Winston could do at home to help him to be less bouncy at school. Things like gardening, carrying heavy books and bouncing whilst wearing a backpack.

She told them both not to worry. Winston was to go home, have a good bounce and a good sleep and be ready for a new school day in the morning.

The next day was Thursday.

Winston was happy as he thought about all the class joining him for the exercise breaks. He had begun to feel quite lonely bouncing around outside while the others were in the classroom.

At the start of the day and before lunch, Mrs Calm encouraged all the pupils to go for a little bounce around the playground. She told them about pupils at another school that had a special racetrack that ran all around the school. Mrs Calm said she would ask Mr White, the Head Teacher, if they could have one of these racetracks too.

Mr White thought it was a wonderful idea and said he would ask the caretaker to start work on it at the weekend.

By Friday, Winston had begun to enjoy school.

It helped him that all the pupils joined in his regular exercise breaks.

He used his timetable to remind himself when he needed to wear the heavy waistcoat, and Mrs Calm got him some heavy pencils and crayons with special grips that made them easy to hold. Winston was also allowed to stand at a higher table to do his work when he wanted to.

That morning, Mrs Calm tested the children on the number work they had been doing.

"I won't bounce, I won't bounce, I won't bounce…just yet," Winston whispered to himself.

He went over to the high table, slipped on his waistcoat and did the number test.

Mrs Calm was very proud of him. She was surprised to see that all the pupils were calmer and quieter after doing the exercises with Winston.

Friday afternoon was sports afternoon and all the families were invited to watch.

Winston joined up with William and Wendy and together they won the relay race. They each got a little medal. Winston's family were so proud.

Daddy Wallaby shouted, "WAY TO GO MY SON!"

Grandpa Wallaby cheered, "WELL DONE! WELL DONE!"

Granny Wallaby's eyes filled with tears of joy,

and Mummy Wallaby proudly cried, "THAT'S MY BOY!"

Winston Wallaby still bounced in the playground,

He still bounced up the stairs,

He still bounced on his bed sometimes,

But now he bounced with care.

He was a wonderful bouncer with energy to burn,

But now he was a wallaby who could finally LEARN!

Coping with Hyperactivity in Children

Toddlers and young children are bundles of energy and frequently flit from one activity to another. However, as children get older their concentration span develops. We are all different – some children take longer to gain control of their emotions and regulate their behaviour than others, and sometimes there might be an underlying cause for this.

Being hyperactive and unable to keep still and concentrate can increase a child's anxiety and they can become depressed, struggling to understand why they find things so difficult and other children do not. This can lead to difficulties at school.

It is also difficult for the people around the child. Parents and teachers can find it very exhausting dealing with a child who is on the move from the moment they wake up to the moment they eventually get to sleep. If they do not understand the reasons for this behaviour, they may become annoyed with the child and think the behaviour is somehow planned to irritate and upset them.

There are many causes of hyperactivity: Attention Deficit Disorder, increased levels of the thyroid hormone, difficulty interpreting sensory information, anxiety and Autism Spectrum Disorder.

SEEKING HELP

If your child is displaying signs of hyperactivity, you should speak to your doctor, who will determine the underlying cause of the symptoms and what type of help your child needs. Depending on the underlying cause, children may be assessed by an occupational therapist and a programme of strategies put in place. Others may be referred for Cognitive Behaviour Therapy, which works on changing thinking patterns, teaching the child how to cope and reduce the effects that hyperactivity can have. Some children may be prescribed drugs to control the symptoms.

It is important to talk to your child's teacher, as hyperactivity can affect the child's ability to learn. Working in partnership with the school will help to develop a consistent approach and enable the school to put strategies in place to help the child to be happy and successful.

School staff may be the first to recognise that the child is hyperactive compared to their classmates. This is because in school more demands are placed on the child to sit still, concentrate and follow the teacher's instructions.

SENSORY DIFFERENCES

We find out about the world through our senses. We need to be able to make sense of the messages coming from the senses.

Receptors in our inner ear give us information about our balance, where our body is in space and what direction it is moving in. If the position of our head changes, messages are sent to the brain. This is called our vestibular sense.

Receptors in muscles, joints and tendons send messages to the brain about our posture and body position. This is called our proprioceptive sense.

Sensory processing difficulties can have a detrimental effect on a child's ability to learn in the classroom environment. If the child does not fully develop the ability to attach meaning to a sensory stimulus the child could display unusual reactions. Many people with autism have described their experiences and difficulties processing information from their senses.

VESTIBULAR DIFFERENCES

The child could be oversensitive to information from the vestibular sense and have a low tolerance for activities that involve changes in the body position. This could result in them being poor at sport and disliking activities that involve spinning or jumping. They may get frightened on escalators. They may have difficulty when running and changing direction quickly. They may have difficulty walking on uneven surfaces.

On the other hand, if the brain does not get enough information from the vestibular sense the child may seek and get pleasure from body movement such as spinning and rocking. They often love playground equipment such as swings and roundabouts and can spin without getting dizzy for extended periods of time. People with autism have described the need for repetitive movement to make themselves calm.

PROPRIOCEPTIVE DIFFERENCES

Hypersensitivity with the proprioceptive sense can mean the child has difficulty controlling fine movements and handling small objects. They may have difficulty dressing and undressing for P.E., tying their shoe laces or doing up buttons. They may also put their body in unusual positions.

Hyposensitivity with the proprioceptive sense can mean children are often unable to interpret signals that tell them where their bodies are in space or to recognise when they are hungry. They can often lean against furniture and people. They may have what is termed as low muscle tone. They may have a tendency to fall over or find it difficult to negotiate a safe route across a room without bumping into furniture or people. They can have little understanding of personal space and may stand too close to others or too far away.

Many children struggle with processing and interpreting sensory information and may seek extra sensory stimulus or avoid sensory activities. Children with sensory difficulties can often become overloaded. Sometimes this results in the child only using one sense at a time, for example taking information from the visual sense but being unable to interpret what is being said to them at the same time. The child may focus on detail and not be able to make sense of the whole situation. They may take longer to switch attention from one sensory stimulus to another as their processing of the information may be delayed. Appropriate activities can help children to get the right amount of information.

SENSORY INTEGRATION

We strongly recommend that the child who is hyperactive is seen by an occupational therapist. Occupational therapists can help by assessing the child and devising a personalised programme of activities that focus on areas of difficulty. Sensory integration works on developing the child's nervous system, regulating the child's alertness and helping them to process information from their senses.

Sensory Integration Therapy is described by Wilkes as "gentle exposure to various sensory stimuli. The aim of this therapy is to strengthen, balance and develop the central nervous system's processing of sensory stimuli."[1]

LEARNING STYLES

We all learn in different ways. Babies learn to connect sensory information with meaning and this enables them to make sense of their environment. The young child needs to move and explore their environment to make sense of it and this is reflected in the design of the Early Years Foundation Stage Curriculum. As children get older and mature their concentration span increases and they are more able to sit still and focus. Older children are expected to sit still for longer and concentrate on tasks for extended periods of time. Some children are not developmentally ready for this.

People have preferred learning styles: some like to learn through watching a demonstration (visual learners), some by listening to information (auditory learners) and others through practical activities (kinaesthetic learners). We want children to be at their most receptive to learn so it is important to identify the child's preferred learning style and incorporate activities using that style into the school day. We all need different things to help us.

THE VALUE OF MOVEMENT

If the child has the need to move and fidget all the time it can be difficult for them to control this and concentrate on anything else. For children who are hyperactive it is not only difficult for them to keep their body still, but their brain may also be overactive. The child can have difficulty regulating their behaviour and be impulsive.

People need varying amounts of movement to maintain concentration. As adults, we may get up and make a coffee, play music, stretch or go and get something to eat. We have worked out strategies to help us complete a task. For many children, we need to be the detective, observe and put strategies in place to help them develop their

---

1   Wilkes, K. (2005) *The Sensory World of the Autistic Spectrum: A Greater Understanding.* London: The National Autistic Society, p.6.

own ways to self-regulate. Activities for kinaesthetic learners, children who need movement and hands-on activities, need careful classroom management, but providing opportunities for movement breaks will enable effective learning. Children with autism are often visual learners and will benefit from the use of visual support such as visual timetables and other visual supports to help them cope with change and transitions from activity to activity.

WHAT IS THE CHILD'S BEHAVIOUR COMMUNICATING?

All behaviour is a form of communication and it is important that we work out the child's needs and introduce alternative activities which meet those needs.

If the child is showing behaviours that indicate the continual need to move and displaying behaviours such as hand flapping or rocking, they may be trying to find a way to calm themselves and organise the sensory information they're processing.

Many people do not appreciate that the child is not behaving in this way to annoy or disrupt others, but is finding it difficult to cope within the environment. The display of undesirable behaviour may be a result of them not being able to process and interpret sensory stimuli.

SUPPORTIVE ACTIVITIES

We have suggested some activities to help the child find coping strategies that remove barriers to learning. We need to show the child appropriate ways to get the extra sensory input they need and crave.

The fun ideas included in this book can be used to help increase attention, body awareness and muscle tone and to help the child regulate their behaviour so they can become calmer and more relaxed. Our aim is that the child will be able to self-regulate and then be ready to learn. Some children may not be developmentally ready to regulate their own emotions, so an understanding adult who is able to help them interpret situations and find coping strategies will be vital to ensure the child can learn in a busy classroom.

Many of these activities are suitable for both home and school use.

Ideas for Helping at Home

There are many things you can do at home to help your child. Understanding your child's behaviour is the first step to helping them.

BECOME A DETECTIVE

Observe and see if you can spot triggers. Does your child become more hyperactive at different times, in different situations or with different people? Spotting patterns to the behaviour and identifying triggers means you will be more able to find ways to help. You can then be proactive and try strategies to prevent the behaviour occurring rather than just reacting to it afterwards. This can give you more confidence.

CALMING ACTIVITIES

Activities that will help to calm the child include whole-body movements – lifting objects, pushing and pulling and actions including sucking, blowing and chewing.

Always encourage the child to do some physical exercise before any activity that requires sustained concentration, such as homework.

- Carrying shopping
- Wearing a backpack with heavy books in it
- Filling a watering can and watering the garden
- Pushing and pulling objects
- Popping bubble wrap
- Digging in the garden
- Hoovering
- Riding a bike
- Riding a scooter
- Rolling pastry
- Jumping and bouncing on the trampoline
- Skipping
- Hopping
- Jumping over rope
- Jumping on bubble wrap
- Marching

- Dancing
- Swimming
- Playing football
- Throwing and catching a ball
- Visiting the playground – swings, climbing ladders, roundabouts, climbing rope walls
- Giving the child a bear hug
- Squeezing a soft toy
- Wrapping the child tightly in a blanket
- Sucking a drink through a straw
- Sucking jelly through a straw
- Drinking from a sports bottle
- Eating chewy foods such as raisins, liquorice, chewing gum
- Biting on a chewy tube
- Blowing up balloons
- Blowing bubbles
- Blowing party blowers
- Blowing a feather with a straw
- Blowing a whistle
- Learning a musical instrument that you need to blow such as a recorder, trumpet or flute

MUSIC

Listening to music can affect our concentration and also be calming. Try a range of music to determine what supports the child.

DEEP PRESSURE

Weighted blankets, weighted backpacks, a weighted toy such as a snake to wrap around the child's shoulders or on their lap or weighted vests are often recommended by occupational therapists. The weight offers gentle pressure that helps to soothe the child and reduce anxiety. Consider the appropriate weight for the physical build of the child, as too much weight could damage joints.

HELPFUL EXERCISES

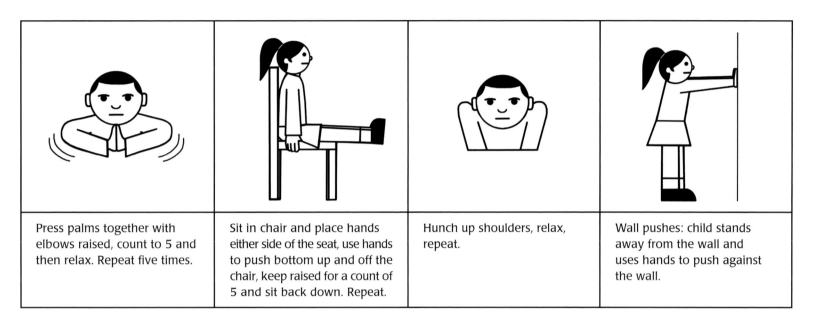

Press palms together with elbows raised, count to 5 and then relax. Repeat five times.	Sit in chair and place hands either side of the seat, use hands to push bottom up and off the chair, keep raised for a count of 5 and sit back down. Repeat.	Hunch up shoulders, relax, repeat.	Wall pushes: child stands away from the wall and uses hands to push against the wall.

ENVIRONMENT

Consider the impact of the environment on the child and create an area they can go to that will support their sensory needs. This could be their bedroom, a pop-up tent or even under the table. Use things to help calm the child such as dimmed lighting, favourite fabrics, mood lights and soft toys. Include a box full of favourite calming activities such as colouring books, comics, bubbles and fidget toys.

Ideas for Helping at School

It is important not to ask the hyperactive child to stop fidgeting and keep still – instead find a reason for them to move that you are in control of.

MANAGING OPPORTUNITIES FOR PUPILS TO MOVE DURING LESSONS

- Many children need to move and fidget. Identify these pupils and choose them to give out equipment, collect in work or take a message to the office.
- Place resources around the room so that pupils have to get up from their seats and collect items at regular intervals rather than just at the start of a lesson.

- Create a designated space that the child can go to if they become sensory overloaded and need to calm down.
- Provide the child with a visual that they can show to take a learning break when they need to.
- Introduce movement breaks for all the children to help them refocus.

Physical activity increases oxygen to the brain. Doing exercises that involve using both sides of the brain can help with large and fine motor control and improve hand–eye coordination.

HELPFUL EXERCISES

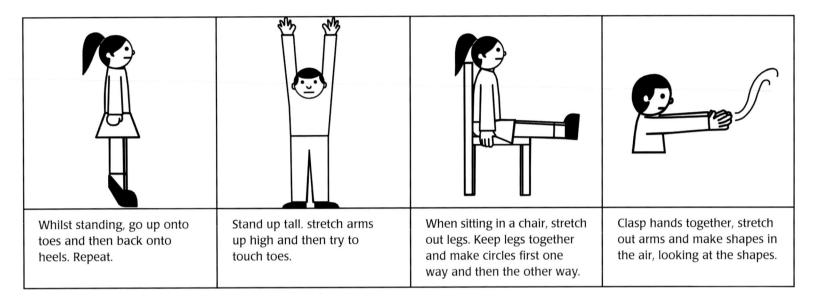

Whilst standing, go up onto toes and then back onto heels. Repeat.	Stand up tall. stretch arms up high and then try to touch toes.	When sitting in a chair, stretch out legs. Keep legs together and make circles first one way and then the other way.	Clasp hands together, stretch out arms and make shapes in the air, looking at the shapes.

Exercises that involve crossing the midline of the body are called laterality exercises. These exercises will help develop motor skills and use different sides of the brain.

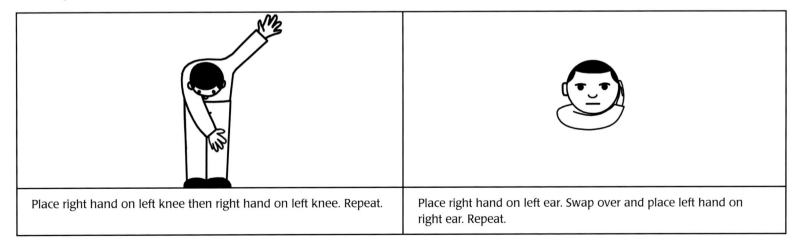

Place right hand on left knee then right hand on left knee. Repeat.	Place right hand on left ear. Swap over and place left hand on right ear. Repeat.

CALMING ACTIVITIES

To help the child to be calm and ready to learn, try introducing some of these activities before the start of a lesson or before a task that requires sustained concentration.

- Moving chairs
- Stacking chairs
- Moving P.E. mats and apparatus
- Rolling playdough
- Using weighted pens and pencils
- Playing "hopscotch"
- Stretching
- Playing the mirror game – create a sequence of movements for the child to copy
- Playing "Simon says"
- Walking along a line
- Playing "follow my leader"
- Catching balloons
- Drinking using a straw
- Drinking using a sports bottle
- Squeezing a stress ball
- Squeezing Blu Tack or Therapeutic Putty
- Using fidget toys – these need to be quiet so as not to distract other children

MAKE A PLAN

Ask the child to identify things they think will help them to calm down. Make a list of activities that the child could refer to when they are beginning to feel anxious.

MY CALMING DOWN STEPS

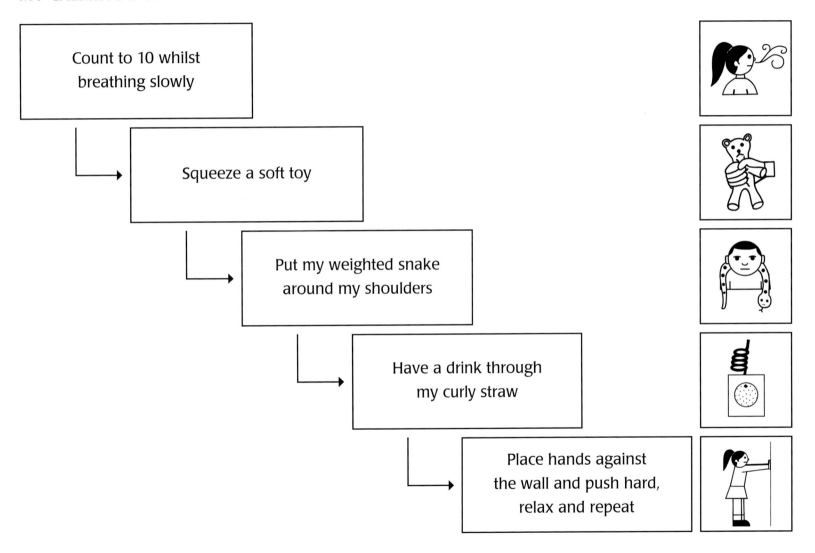

Count to 10 whilst breathing slowly

Squeeze a soft toy

Put my weighted snake around my shoulders

Have a drink through my curly straw

Place hands against the wall and push hard, relax and repeat

SET UP ACTIVITY CIRCUITS

This could involve hopping, jumping, balancing on a bench or setting up lines of cones for the child to run around and change direction.

Use P.E. activities to develop spatial awareness – encourage moving over, through and under, throwing and catching beanbags or balls or aiming beanbags into a hoop.

CONSIDER THE ENVIRONMENT

Look at the placing of tables, cupboards, bookcases, etc. to avoid them becoming obstacles that the child may fall over or knock over.

CONSIDER THE SEATING

Check chairs are the correct height in relation to the table to make it a comfortable working space. Be flexible about where the child does their work – perhaps the child could be allowed to stand to do their work or work at a high table. Use carpet squares to indicate where the child should sit when they are sitting on the floor for an activity.

USE VISUALS TO SUPPORT THE CHILD

Children with autism are often very reliant on visual supports; these can also be very helpful for the whole class. For example, a large whole-class visual timetable will help all the children to understand and follow the structure of the day.

For the child who is hyperactive, activities can be broken down and movement breaks can be scheduled into their timetable. This can be represented on a visual strip so that the child can remove the image when they have completed the task.

EXAMPLE OF A VISUAL SCHEDULE TO SHOW MOVEMENT BREAKS BETWEEN ACTIVITIES

| reading | movement break | writing | movement break | number work | movement break |

GIVE WARNINGS OF TRANSITIONS

Transitions can be very stressful, particularly for the child with autism who likes routine and for things to be predictable. Warn the child about any changes to the routine of the day or changes in staffing. Using visuals can help to do this as they are tangible and the pupil can continually refer to them for reassurance.

TEACH PERSONAL SPACE

This is the physical space between you and another person. If someone is standing too close we often feel uncomfortable. However, the distance that feels comfortable between ourselves and another person varies according to factors such as how well you know the person, how much you like and trust the person and the situation – for example, we often accept standing closer than we normally would in busy places such as the tube or a lift. Some children find it difficult to recognize when they are being "space invaders" and standing too close.

Explain the term "personal space" to the child and practise the appropriate distance to stand away from others in a variety of situations.

Resources

MOVEMENT BREAK SYMBOLS

EXERCISE SYMBOLS

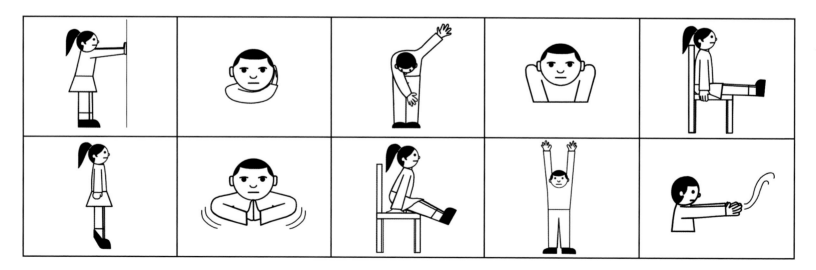

MY CALMING DOWN STEPS

Write in the boxes what helps you to become calm.

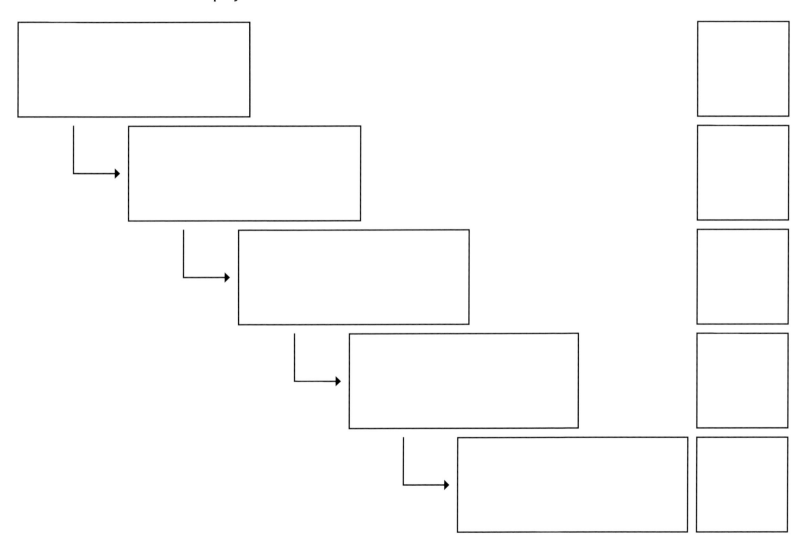

Joy Beaney, MA, has many years' experience in both mainstream and special education. During her career she has been an Assistant Head at a special school and manager of an Inclusion Support Service that provided staff training and support for children with autism in mainstream schools. Joy lectures at Brighton University delivering their Postgraduate Certificate in Autism. Joy has published books including *Autism in the Primary Classroom*, *Autism in the Secondary Classroom* and *Creating Autism Champions*. Joy set up 'Autism Train', which promotes and shares best practice through providing training on aspects of autism.

Haitham Al-Ghani is a book illustrator and cartoon animator. He graduated with Triple Distinction in Multi Media Studies and was awarded the Vincent Lines Award for creative excellence.

K.I. Al-Ghani is a specialist advisory teacher, autism trainer and inclusion consultant with over 40 years of experience in education.

Kay is currently a specialist teacher for inclusion support and is involved with training professionals, students and parents in all aspects of ASD. As an author and a mother of a son with ASD – the illustrator Haitham Al-Ghani – she has spent the last 28 years researching the enigma that is autism.

Kay is also a part-time lecturer at Brighton University, delivering their Postgraduate Certificate in Autism. Kay is an international author of many ASD-related books published by Jessica Kingsley Publishers, including bestseller *The Red Beast: Controlling anger in children with Asperger Syndrome*.